How I Met My Monster

Written by
Amanda Noll

Illustrated by
Howard McWilliam

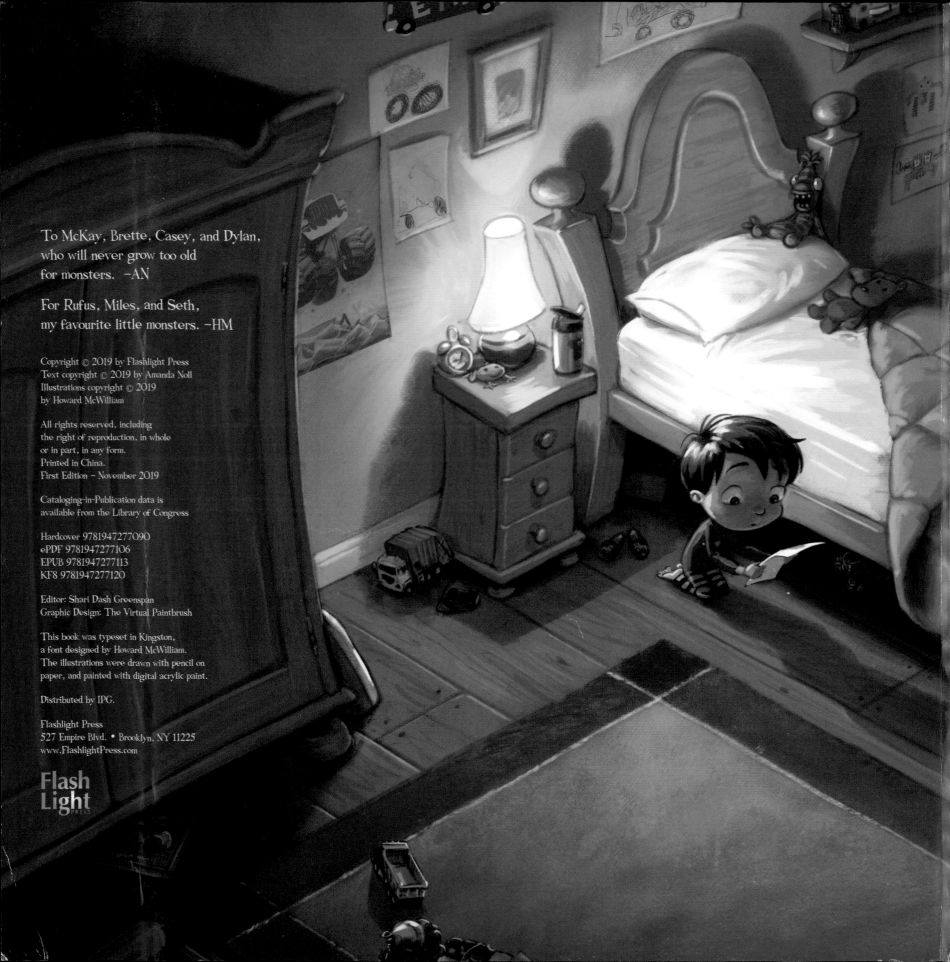

Copyright © 2019 by Flashlight Press
Text copyright © 2019 by Amanda Noll
Illustrations copyright © 2019
by Howard McWilliam

All rights reserved, including
the right of reproduction, in whole
or in part, in any form.
Printed in China.
First Edition – November 2019

Cataloging-in-Publication data is
available from the Library of Congress

Hardcover 9781947277090
ePDF 9781947277106
EPUB 9781947277113
KF8 9781947277120

Editor: Shari Dash Greenspan
Graphic Design: The Virtual Paintbrush

This book was typeset in Kingston,
a font designed by Howard McWilliam.
The illustrations were drawn with pencil on
paper, and painted with digital acrylic paint.

Distributed by IPG.

Flashlight Press
527 Empire Blvd. • Brooklyn, NY 11225
www.FlashlightPress.com

Flash
Light
PRESS

One night, when I reached
under the bed for my truck,
I found this note instead.

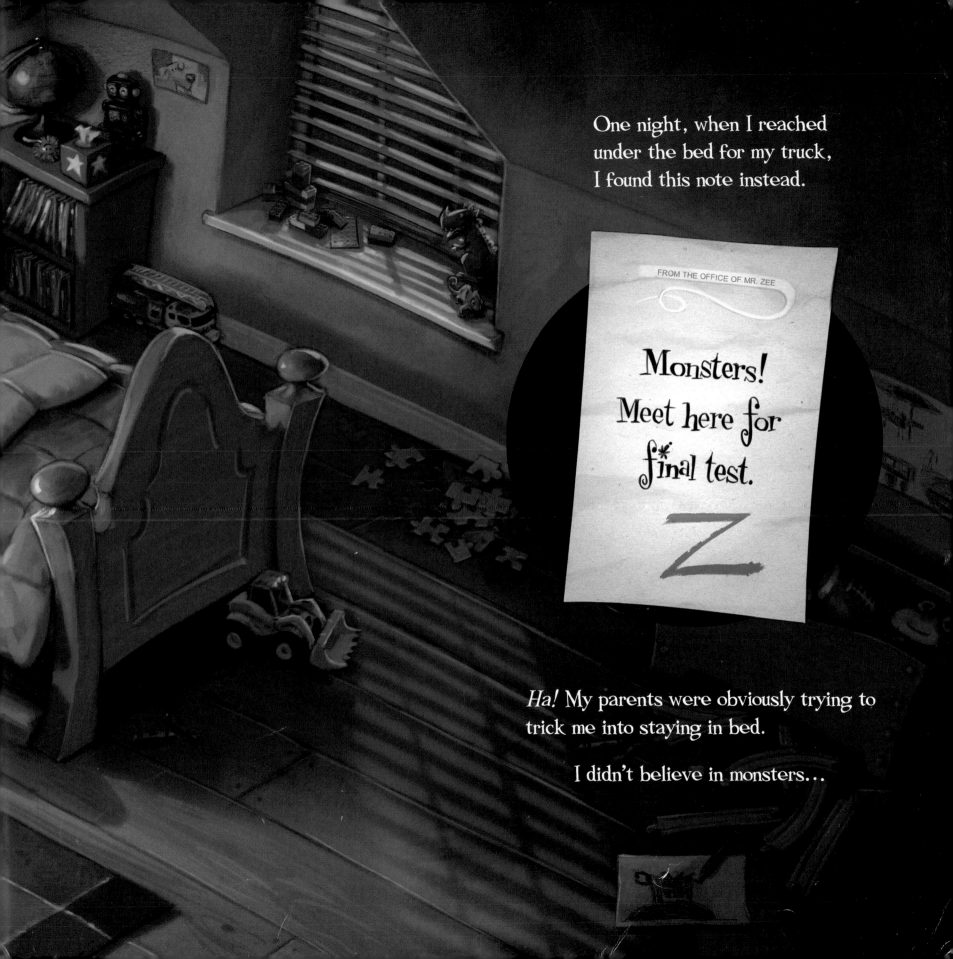

FROM THE OFFICE OF MR. ZEE

Monsters!
Meet here for
f*inal test.

Z

Ha! My parents were obviously trying to
trick me into staying in bed.

I didn't believe in monsters…

...so I crumpled the paper, grabbed my truck, and zipped over to my garage.

I heard some creaking and rumbling, but I wasn't scared. Our house always made noises at night.

But then a voice under the bed scolded,
"Stop that stomach rumbling!
The child will hear you."

Voices? Stomach rumbling?
If this was part of
my parents' trick,
it was pretty cool.

I peered into the inky blackness. Five pairs of eyes
blinked back.

"See? Now he knows we're here," the voice sighed.
"One of you has broken Monster Rule Number 1:
Maintain the element of surprise."

This is no trick, I thought. *There ARE monsters under my bed!*

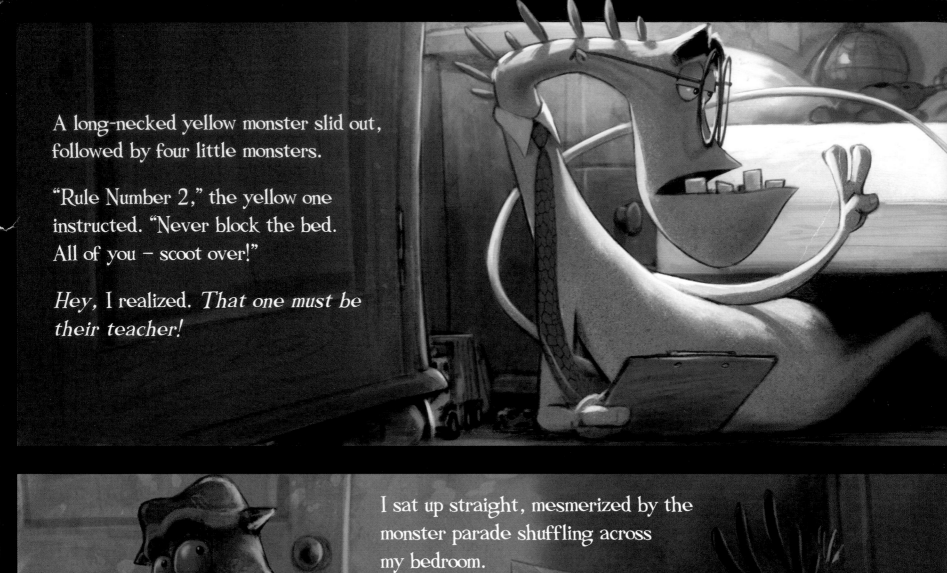

A long-necked yellow monster slid out, followed by four little monsters.

"Rule Number 2," the yellow one instructed. "Never block the bed. All of you – scoot over!"

Hey, I realized. *That one must be their teacher!*

I sat up straight, mesmerized by the monster parade shuffling across my bedroom.

"That's better," the teacher-monster said. "Access to the bed is clear. Now, who knows Rule Number 3?"

The purple monster teetered on his tiptoes and gurgled, "Get the child into bed!"

"That's correct, Genghis. And how would you do that?"

"Well, Mr. Zee, I would… roar my scariest roar!"

"Alright, give it a go."

Genghis took a deep breath, opened his mouths, and let out a tiny *blurp!*

"Stomach rumbling would have a better chance of getting me into bed than *that* funny little noise," I laughed.

"The child is right," said Mr. Zee, shaking his head. "That was not sufficiently scary. Genghis, I'm sorry. You're not the best monster for this child."

There was some creaking as Genghis slunk beneath the bed.

Before I could investigate
where Genghis had gone, Mr. Zee asked,
"NOW who wants to try to get the child into bed?"

The orange monster looked at the ceiling and the red monster
looked at the floor. Only the green one looked at me.
First, he stared at my toes and started drooling. Then he
took a step toward me, and I heard that rumbling noise again.

I sprang into bed so he couldn't get my feet.

Mr. Zee blinked. "Very unconventional, Gabe. Your stomach gurgles seem to be what this child needs."

What I *needed* was to make sure this little Gabe-monster didn't eat my toes!

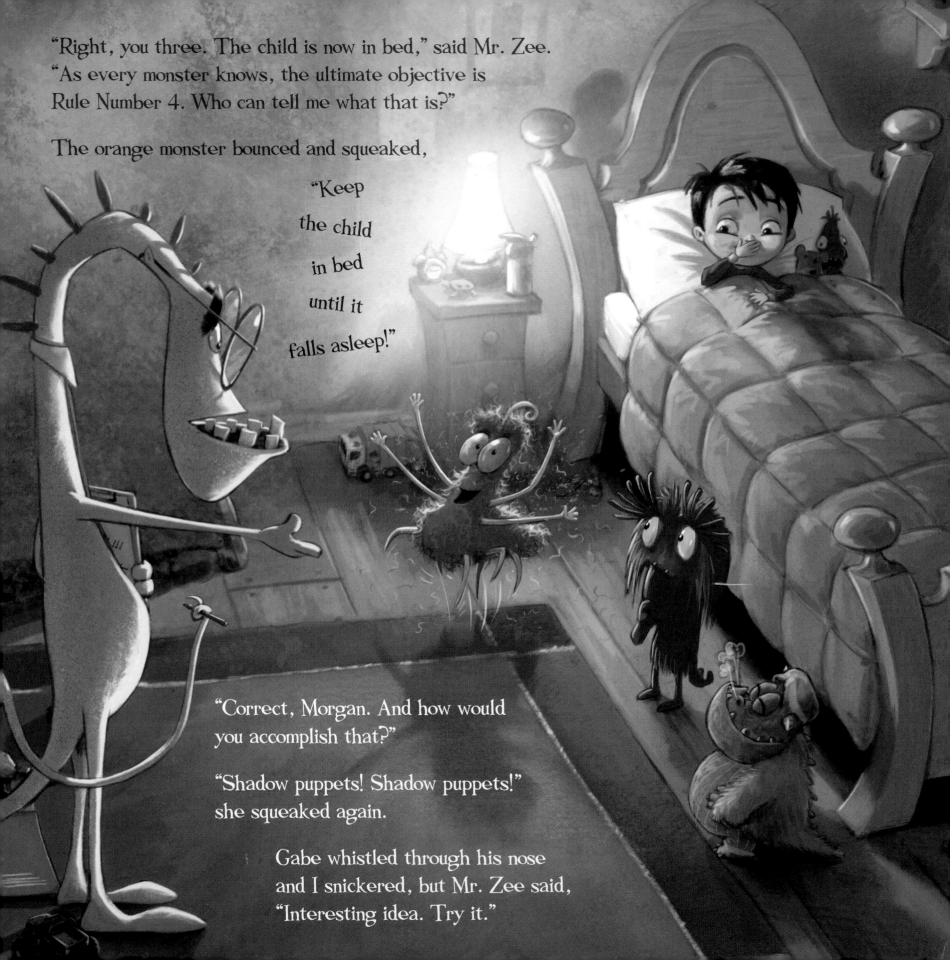

"Right, you three. The child is now in bed," said Mr. Zee. "As every monster knows, the ultimate objective is Rule Number 4. Who can tell me what that is?"

The orange monster bounced and squeaked,

"Keep

the child

in bed

until it

falls asleep!"

"Correct, Morgan. And how would you accomplish that?"

"Shadow puppets! Shadow puppets!" she squeaked again.

Gabe whistled through his nose and I snickered, but Mr. Zee said, "Interesting idea. Try it."

Morgan hopped onto my night table and flailed her arms near my lamp. Silly shadows blobbed onto the wall, and a cloud of fluffy fur tickled my nose.

"AAAAACHOOOO!"

"Morgan, stop at once," Mr. Zee ordered. "You're supposed to *scare* him – not make him *sneeze!* I'm sorry, but you're not a match either."

Morgan's arms flopped to her sides and she scuttled under my bed. There was some more creaking, and Morgan was gone.

After all that sneezing I really needed a tissue.
Suddenly, a huge shadow of uncut claws
loomed across my room.

Awesome! I thought.
And kind of scary.
I froze in place.

"Powerful performance, Gabe," said Mr. Zee, "but do either of you see a problem?"

"Ooh, I know!" chirped the red monster. "The child is out of bed again!"

"Correct, Abigail," Mr. Zee continued, "and one of you must get him back in. Let's revisit Rule Number 1: Maintain the element of surprise."

All at once – POOF! – the monsters vanished. Then I heard more rumbling. *Were they hiding in my closet making noises to scare me?*

Ha! No! It was only my stomach grumbling. All this excitement was making me hungry!

I tiptoed past the closet and peeked out the door.

So far, so good.
No monsters.

Then I stepped over the squeaky stair and sneaked down to the kitchen.

As I reached into the pantry,
I heard some chattering behind me.
I sure hoped it wasn't that toe-loving Gabe.

I yanked open the fridge.
Ha! It wasn't Gabe! It was just the
red monster, shivering on the shelf.

"Found you!" I laughed.

"Nice try, Abigail," said Mr. Zee, "but this isn't working. You're not the right monster for this child."

"But Mr. Zee," she whined, "it's not *my* fault he's not scared of me."

"I'm sorry, Abigail. Let's go."

Abigail clomped behind Mr. Zee.

When I heard the creaking, I knew she was gone.

I grabbed some crackers and headed upstairs, wondering if Gabe was gone too.

I munched all the way down the hall....

When I opened the door a minute later......

… then went into the bathroom to brush my teeth again.

… Gabe was definitely NOT gone!

He was right there –
and he was
HUGE!

I charged into my room and slammed the door.
When I leaped into bed, I knew my toes were safe. *Whew!*

I was surprised to hear
breathing under my bed.
Ragged breathing.
And stomach rumbling.

"Hey, kid," Gabe growled.
"Good to see ya."

I pulled my covers up tight.

"Now if you don't mind,
I'd like to start the evening
with an ominous puddle
of drool."

I peeked over the edge
of the bed. Green ooze
spread soundlessly
from underneath.

Then the bed quivered
as Gabe unfurled
his spiked tail.

"Well, this looks quite promising," Mr. Zee noted.

When I heard some more creaking,
I knew Mr. Zee was gone.

I was alone… with Gabe.

Gabe loomed over my bed and began sharpening his uncut claws on my bedpost.

"H-How'd you get so big?" I gasped.

"Rule Number 5, my friend," he explained.
"People food makes monsters grow.
So thanks for the crackers.
Got any toes I can munch?"

I scrunched in my feet so Gabe couldn't get them.
This was WAY better than playing with trucks.

Gabe dove for it. His soft, comforting snorts
filled the room as he snuffled the toy.

I shivered.

"Kid, I think this is the beginning of a beautiful friendship."

"No other monster
can scare me like you!"
I giggled.